Unopened Presents

by Charlotte McKee

Elm Grove Publications

Waco, Texas

ISBN # 978-0-9905977-8-0

Elm Grove Publications
Waco, Texas
https://www.elmgrovepub.com

Dedicated to the memory of
my husband
Danny McKee
Without his love and encouragemnet
this book could not have been written.

Table of Contents

Unopened Presents

The Empty Branch on My Family Tree

chapter 1

"Ivy Calloway!" Jason calls my name first for Red Rover because I know how to hold on tight. I'm the oldest girl in school, until Teah came. She's my best friend, but she's not here today for morning recess. By after lunch recess my life changed forever. My friends looked away from me. Some gave me long, questioning stares.

The teacher had pointed to the empty branch on my family tree assignment. She asked, "Ivy, you don't know your grandmother's name?"

Every eye in sixth grade turned and burned into me.

"Sure, I know. Grandma Calloway and Mima Kelly."

"Not those two," the teacher said slowly like I couldn't hear. "Your mother's mother. Do you know her name?"

I shook my head.

"That's odd," the teacher said to herself.

My classmate's eyes opened even wider.

Family Tree

???
____
grandmother's name

"Didn't you think that was strange?" The teacher asked.

"No. My mom never talked about it." A herd of wild horses turned loose in my head.

"And you don't think that was strange? Here."

The teacher handed me back my homework. "Take this home and let your mother fill it out."

****

"Do I have another grandmother?" I call to Mom. I run into our front yard. "By my math, I'm short a grandmother. I'm sure. I can count on my fingers. They don't call me the fastest fingers in sixth grade for nothing."

"Why so greedy for grannies all of a sudden?" Mom asks. A floppy hat shades her face. She twists my question around into her question. She doesn't answer it. "You have two grannies -- Grandma Calloway and now Mima Kelly since Steve and I married. Most everyone has two. How many more grannies do you want, Ivy?"

"I only want what's mine," I say.

When I ask Mom questions about family, she starts talking fast. Now she's talking Mighty Mouse fast. I can't tell what's true and what's not.

Her voice fills with pride when she says, "You are Mima Kelly's granddaughter. Her oldest son, Steve's, third wife's child from a previous marriage."

"Sounds great when you say it like that," I say. Talking about family makes Mom nervous or sad or mad, so I'm careful what I say. But I'm desperate. I need a name.

"Mom, the fact is I don't have any roots. I don't go back very far. I have Old Dad—Charlie, who you swore I would keep even after you married Steve when I was four. New Dad and Old Dad. That's how you explained it."

"Ivy," Mom eyes me. She's glad to change the subject away from her family.

"You didn't lose your Old Dad," she says. "You'll have him forever. Nothing can change that."

"I know, Mom." I like the idea of having two dads. With Old Dad, I didn't feel like I had one. I wrote my two grandpa's names on the branches of my family tree. They passed away.

I look at Mom as she kneels to pull a weed. She digs her fingernails down into the dirt, twists her hand, and then comes up with a long root.

People say Mom and I look exactly alike. They're nuts, of course. We are both skinny. I have her bony hands and feet. But that's all. She has freckles, and I don't. Her brown hair flips up. My dishwater blond hair hangs down. She has a nice long nose. Mine turns up at the tip like Old Dad's. But where do I get these deep brown eyes?

Old Dad is a blue-gray eyed handsome man. That's what Grandma Calloway always says. And he comes from a long line of blue-grey eyes. They're not the same as mine. His eyes are more squinted and pointed at the ends. I don't get my brown eyes from Mom either. Her eyes are as green as her garden. I feel alone, and different, unlike my family.

Mom stands up and tosses her little weed into a pile. She shakes her muddy finger at me like Grandma Calloway always does. "Young ladies should do this and that."

"Grandma doesn't get me," I laugh at Mom's impersonation. "She does have a lot of "should"! Thank goodness she moved away. I know she sent me nice dresses when I was little. But like I would ever wear one!"

"You did. I have pictures," Mom says. She rests in the speckled shade of the pecan tree that covers our front yard. "But they weren't dresses to play soccer in."

"Soccer! The greatest game in the world!" I announce. I wear jeans and tennis shoes most of the time. You never know. I might suddenly get a chance to play soccer.

Grandma Calloway doesn't share my enthusiasm. By the look on her face, I get the idea she wants to hold me down and stuff pink lace up my nose.

"Mima Kelly likes me the way I am," I tell mom.

Then comes that question again, the question that has taken years to form in the back of my head now wants to be asked out loud. Ask it! I tell myself. Bet I won't get a straight answer from Mom.

Ask it anyway!

So, I do. "If Grandma Calloway is Old Dad's mom, and Mima Kelly is New Dad's mom, where's your mother?"

Mom opens her mouth to speak, and nothing comes out. Her lips move and then she smiles, yawning into the sunshine, "Well, I like you too, Ivy Calloway, just the way you are."

She quickly gathers her weeds and dashes off like I haven't just asked her the most important question of my life.

I catch up with her as she dumps her bundle onto the compost pile out back. "We're doing family trees in school," I tell her. "I need to know your mother's name. It goes on the empty line above your name. My teacher asked me if you are an orphan! I don't know if you are or not. You've never said."

Mom looks at me like she's trying to answer. "I can't," she says and just slams her hoe into the compost and heads for the front yard.

"Mom!" I run up to her as the sun slips behind a cloud. I whisper, "The teacher said if I have a grandmother, her name belongs on this line, or I'll have to write UNKNOWN there."

"That would be nice." Mom is not paying attention. She squints as the sun comes out again.

"Why don't you get started on your chores, Ivy?"

Mom is keeping a secret.

I don't have any chores right after school except homework. And this assignment is becoming a chore! Why would anyone hide a mother? Now, I don't care if I make Mom mad or what.

I say. "Tomorrow is the last day of the assignment, "I must know today." Then the question just spills out. "Mom, did you have a mother?"

She turns and leans on her hoe. When she nods, her hat bobs and a shadow slips over her eyes. She's hiding something under her hat.

"Of course, I had a mother, Ivy. Every creature has a mother," she whispers.

Unreal. "I know that. But you never mentioned one. I'm eleven years old, and I don't remember you talking about your mother. Not once."

"Well," Mom props the hoe against the tree and sits on the grass, "I did have a mother."

"Is she alive?" I gasp and clutch my hands together. I'm begging for this grandmother.

"Oh," Mom raises her eyebrows and answers slowly, "Very much so. Her name is Molly Bell."

"Do you know where Molly Bell is?" I ask, my voice rising. I'm pacing back and forth.

"Uh-huh." Mom says. She sits down and looks up at me, hugging her knees. "Is this a school assignment? Go-Home-and-Grill-your-Mom Day?"

"Well, yes, no, but why haven't I met her before?" I twist a lock of hair, pulling it tight. "She's my grandmother! I should get to meet her."

Mom reaches up and tugs on my tee shirt. "Sit, Ivy."

"Maybe she doesn't know about me?" I ask as I drop my backpack. I plop down on the grass beside her and fiddle a stick through a small hole in my jeans making it bigger.

"She knows," Mom answers.

My chest squeezes the air out of my lungs. "Why haven't you told me about her?"

Mom leans over her knees and her eyes gleam with tears. She says, "I thought I was doing you a favor."

"Then, she doesn't love me?" I pull the stick out of my jeans and throw it. The tightness spreads to my throat.

"She doesn't know you," Mom smiles. "If she did, she'd spoil you rotten and buy you pres-ents."

"Then why don't we go see her?" I knew my new grandmother would be someone who "gets" me and laughs at my stories. I see her just waiting to spoil me. I could see piles of unopened presents.

I stop unwrapping presents in my mind when Mom answers: "It's me she doesn't love."

Loosing at the Game of Game of Love

chapter 2

Mom's words stick in my head like planted seeds. I cover them up and pat them down with a lot of questions. Why doesn't Mom's mother love her? What did Mom do?

Then I water her words by telling Teah, my best friend at school, about it. We're always together. We both love climbing the same tree. Our heads and secrets we keep hidden in the branches. Teah is so wise.

"Liking comes first," she says. "Love follows."

During recess we climb up and watch Michael and Jason. I forget about my mysterious grandmother for a while, and we just hang out.

I think I have boys all figured out. Michael and Jason have been my boyfriends for years-the smartest and cutest boys in school. Michael is blond and can sing. When we play baseball, we can be close but not get in each other's way. Jason is tall and dark. He loves archeology, so we dig. He's Indiana Jones.

But things change in September.

Amy steals Michael away from me. That's Amy of the golden curls and ribbons everywhere. Sure, she's pretty, but she looks too much like Miss Piggy for me. She's selfish, too. One by one she has stolen everybody's boyfriends, and now she has Michael.

Jason and I go on and play our game. He's Indy and I'm his girlfriend, Marion. We dig and he draws pictures of things we collect—arrowheads, bones and pieces of glass and steel. Then I write stories about each one of them.

"Found that lost city yet?" Michael jeers down at us. Amy stands beside him and giggles.

"You're stepping on our dig sight!" Jason blasts.

Normally, Jason is quiet and fun. He isn't much of a fighter, so I must do most of it for him. He takes teasing for that, so I must fight some more.

"Why else do you think we'd rope it off?" I yell back at Michael. I stand there, facing him with my hands on my hips.

"It's the Game of Love, Ivy," Teah says later in our tree. I tilt my head for a better listen. But, why has Michael stopped playing it with me? Am I not lovable? I loved him, but he stopped loving me. What did I do wrong?

Then, I turn to Teah and say, "I'm skinny. I don't have enough of what Aimee has, plenty of. Boobs!"

Teah nods. Her branch twitches.

It's not fair! I try to tell Michael and Jason, "Those are not real! It's baby fat! Her tight belt pushes the fat up into her bra." That's the magic word—bra. She wears one and I don't.

Michael stomps our dig sight and Amy cheers. Jason and I fight the villains, wins and start digging somewhere else.

I'm glad Amy can't take Jason away from me. Jason never seems interested in her. That alone is enough to make her hunt him down. So, Amy stalks him. One day she lures him out of the dirt, and it's not long before she tries to kiss him.

Then in a blur of fists, Michael slams into Jason and pins him to the ground. Michael pounds him with short jabs to the stomach. Michael screams, "No!" and keeps on punching.

I must pull Michael off. "That's enough, Michael! Jason's lips are turning blue!"

My heart breaks. Blue or not, Jason's lips soon swear love for Amy. I lose Jason, too. I think for sure I'll spend the rest of sixth grade in this oak tree, watching my two ex-boyfriends fight over Amy.

Every day they play Amy's game, Lady Gets a Valentine. The object of her game is to choose one. Only Amy never chooses. Michael and Jason take turns knocking on her door. First one then the other throws himself at her. Michael sings, "Come and Knock on my Door," from Three's Company. Then Jason falls on his knees right in the play yard and recites some stupid poem.

"I can't stand to look at Jason on his knees one more time! I could puke!" I say to Teah later. I want to think about some Game of Love that I'm not losing. So, I wonder about my mysterious grandmother. Mom said she would love me if she knew me. I say, "I want to know her!"

Teah says, "Let's celebrate!" She jumps out of the tree and runs across the play yard taking me with her. "I hope she's as great as my Nana."

Later back in our tree I ask Teah, "I wonder what my mom did to make my grandma stop loving her? Love can stop. Michael stopped loving me? Could love stop? Could someone else stop loving me like Michael did? Could my mom?"

"I didn't know mothers could do that—stop loving, I mean," Teah says from the branches. "Mom's love. That's their job. That's what they do, Ivy."

"My mom keeps a secret," I tell her. "And I know it makes her sad. This morning I caught her crying."

"What about?"

"No reason I could tell," I say. "When she saw me, she jumped up and attacked a basket of towels. She folded them by karate chops, and I pretended not to see. Maybe if I put her and my new grandmother together again, Mom would be happy, and I'd have
another grandmother."

"With presents!" Teah says.

The bell rings, I run home not even looking back for Jason. We don't run any more. He waits for Amy. They're having ice cream together.
I can't think about that now.

I'm thinking about my mom. What made her mother stop loving her? How does love stop? What would I have to do to make my mom stop loving me? Do I really want to know?

As soon as I hit the front door, I must ask Mom, "Is there something you did to make your mother stop loving you?"

Mom follows me through the kitchen and into my room. I plop down cross-legged into my yellow beanbag chair.

Mom answers, "What could I have possibly done? I was a two-years old baby. I was Granny's baby. She rocked me. She fed me. I thought I belonged to her. One day Mother just showed up in the kitchen. She wore a smile and an apron and was helping Granny with breakfast. I wondered, what is she doing here?"

"Where had she been?" I ask.

"She lived there with Granny, too, but I hadn't really noticed her until that day. It was the same day a soldier jumped up on Granny's front porch. He ignored everyone else and ran straight toward me, tossing away his soldier's hat. Then he grabbed me and whooped. To my horror, he threw me up in the air, too, and caught me as I came screaming down.

"Lulu, meet your father," my mother said.

"My parents took me away and we moved to Houston. I felt kidnapped. I didn't know these people or why I was with them. There was these people or why I was with them. There was no more sunshine. "A year later Mom was pregnant."

When she was ready to go to the hospital, my parents dropped me off at Granny's. I was thrilled to be back. I thought I'd come home. Aunts and uncles were there waving goodbye and shouting as my parents drove away in a cloud of dust. I hoped this meant forever. To make sure they stayed gone for good, I gathered rocks and threw them at the car.

Let Bygones
Be Gone

chapter 3

"So you lived with your granny?"

"No, no," Mom says. "I was only there long enough for Mother to go to the hospital and deliver her baby, my sister, Holly."

"Holly? She's my Aunt Holly," I marvel. This is all coming together for me.

Mom says, "When I threw those rocks, my aunts and uncles changed. From that day on they saw me as confused; not knowing which way was up. I paid for my tantrum. I became the family dingbat. When the dumb blonde jokes came around, I used them. I bleached my hair blond and pursed my lips together. I opened my eyes wide and learned how to look stupid." Mom laughs, "I could always make my family laugh even if they were laughing at me."

She turns to me. "Ivy, you made me remember something. I thought all this time I'd done nothing. Not true. I did throw those rocks!"

Later in the kitchen mom comes up with the idea of cooking potatoes. I get the big pot and put the potatoes in it. Smashing potatoes with the skins on is my favorite job.

"Daddy has invited me, all of us, to come to Cotton Moon, Texas, for Christmas. Right or wrong, he's an old man. This could be his last Christmas."

I have a grandpa! I think, but... my grandpa's last Christmas?

Mom says, "Ivy, if we were to go back, I wouldn't expect a grand family reunion."

"And, why not?" I ask. "That's what I want, a grand family reunion!"

Mom flinches. "My daddy has asked for me. He doesn't have much longer to live. He's run out of time. That's the reason I'd go. And for you, Ivy, I'd go for you. You could meet your grandpa before it's too late."

Too late for what? I wonder.

I can imagine grandpa and me walking hand in hand, our fishing poles resting on our shoulders. We'd sing some old country songs, and I'd splash my toes in the water.

Mom says, "You have a grandpa, and he has said,"Let's let bygones be bygones."

I open my mouth to ask what bygones are. But I think I know. Bygones are about a long ago past, like memories, like the yesterdays before I was born. All I know about my new, alive grandpa is that he wants the bygones to be gone. They must make him sad. I want them gone, too. I ask, "How sick is grandpa?"

"He has emphysema and a heart condition," Mom says. "His doctor has told him to get his affairs in order."

How do you get your affairs in order? A grandfather I don't know is about to die. How much time does he have?

Then mom seems to slip away almost whispering. She talks fast, "My mother called today. I talked to her and my sister on the phone. They talked about Christmas. Everything sounded so friendly. They're talking get-together," Mom says then suddenly darkens. "I just hope it's not a trap!"

The hairs stand up on the back of my neck. I bristle like Skoshi does when she barks. Just talking about these people makes Mom cry. But I wouldn't let anyone trap her. I'd be there to watch out for her. If we went maybe I would discover who gave me my deep brown eyes. I could go and find out that. "You talked to Grandma?"

Mom twitches a smile at me then continues. "Said they would love to meet you and Steve. My sister has remarried. Her son, your cousin Ernie Gene, is a freshman in high school. He plays the drums and has won a band jacket this year. Maybe it could be different this time."

"I have a cousin? How come it needs to be different this time?"

Every answer makes more questions.

Mom throws her hands up. "Because each time we get together it gets worse! The last time was in court, twelve years ago."

"Court?" I ask. First I've heard of court.

Mom says, "When my sister Holly left her husband in Fort Worth, she took the baby but did not pick up her four-year-old son from day care."

"I have two cousins?" I ask.

Mom nods. "Later Holly returned with a lawyer, Mother's little brother, Uncle Jake, to get back the four-year-old she left. I was subpoenaed by Holly's husband. When it was my time to speak, my parents cast me hard looks and left the courtroom. I told the judge my mother and sister could not mother a cat together. Uncle Jake, with Holly in his ear, questioned me for an hour. They tried to discredit me.

"In the end, Holly lost her son. By the time the judge wacked his gavel down, I was through, too. I didn't ever want to see any of them again!"

Dad joins us in the kitchen. "Cheese, Louise! These potatoes are ready! Are you boiling them on high?"

Then, he looks at Mom and touches her shoulder. "Lou, I could hear you all over the house. Your daddy wants to forgive and forget. Maybe it's time to see them again. Maybe we all need to start over and let bygones be bygones."

Mom jumps, grabs the pot, and dumps steam in the sink. "No, he doesn't!" she says. "Mother bullies him! He does what she says. Not once did Daddy stand up for me, never once. Certainly not in court!" Mom starts crying.

I hate it when she cries. It makes my stomach hurt. Only a kid is supposed to cry. When adults cry, it means something is really bad wrong.

"My Dear!" Dad says to Mom. "I think your parents are trying to apologize, to say they care and want to make it up to you."

"I think so, too, Mom," I say. I can feel my heart beating.

Mom sets down the pot of potatoes. She blows air out between her teeth. "Ivy, smash these," she tells me.

I get the milk and butter out of the fridge.

Dad hands me the smasher. "Don't over-smash."

"I know. I know. Leave some chunks." Dad likes the creamy with the rough. You can tell by his big stomach that he loves smashed potatoes with the skins on almost as much as I do.

Dad says, "Lou, that old man who came here and cried on our front porch loves you. You were lost and your Daddy came and found you."

"What old man?" I ask. Then I remembered one day a long time ago. I came home from school and found Mom and Dad talking with an old man on the front porch. I thought he was a painter or gardener looking for work. He saw me and said I was pretty.

"If Daddy looked for me, it's because Mother sent him for some devilish purpose!"

Tears glisten in her eyes.

Why did Mom's Daddy have to find her? Has she been lost all this time? I don't understand. But I remembered that old man, and he didn't seem the kind who would carry out a devilish purpose. "Maybe he just wanted to see you," I say.

"I wish it could be so simple," Mom says.

"It is that simple, Lou," Dad says.

He twists the brass pepper mill and cracks pepper over the potatoes.

I'm still thinking about Mom lost as we sit down at the table. How can she be lost? This is her house. She's here.

I ask, "Was that old man my grandpa?"

"Yes, Ivy."

"Then, let's go," I say. I think I would do anything to go see my new family. I could make sure nothing happens to Mom.

Grandpa's Last Christmas

chapter 4

October comes with a few chills and a new coat. Some days I wear long underwear under my jeans to school. Mostly it's hot by afternoon, and I forget my coat and stuff the long underwear in my book bag.

"Is my grandmother's town bigger than Fort Worth?" I ask Mom.

She says, "Cotton Moon is a two-acre town site on the edge of a canyon. Once, this land was full of buffalo and covered with tall grass, flowing in waves like a giant ocean. It's all cotton fields and country roads, now."

"You lived on a farm?" I ask.

"No," Mom says. "I was a townie. My friends rode the school bus up and down the canyon every day. They knew those country roads. I only knew the streets in town—three churches, a school, a cotton gin, a museum and a Dairy Queen."

That's all? I'm a metro-plex girl. I've never stopped in a small town before, just passed through. What do they do for fun in Cotton Moon?

November comes with freezing rain. I don't forget my coat anymore. Mom adds scarves and gloves to remember to bring home, and I forget those.

Part of my plan is to keep Cotton Moon on Mom's mind until she decides to let me go visit my grandmother.

The next day in school, I pull up a computer printout. I can hardly wait. I show my research to Mom that night.

In 1903 a cowboy from the Jones Livestock Company pulled the heel of his boot over the dirt, making an X. "This will be Cotton Moon," he said.

"That's good, Ivy," Mom says. "Read a little further on. Recently, there were dinosaur bones found in the canyon."

I'll go back and check that. If I could dig, Jason would be so jealous. He has a shelf of bones in his room. I only have some pterodactyl teeth I picked up at Glen Rose.

Maybe now is the right time for my big pitch to Mom. This could be the chance to meet my new grandmother and find a dinosaur bone to beat Jason with.

Here goes. "Grandmother is mad at you, Mom, right? Not at me? Listen, I've been on buses. I rode one to Austin and one to Glen Rose last year. I've gone hundreds of miles. If you really don't want to see grandmother, I could go by myself. I could ride the bus to Cotton Moon."

Mom answers, "You rode with your class and teachers to Austin, and you were with friends going to Glen Rose. You think I would let you go to Cotton Moon alone?"

My anger busts out. "I'm old enough to take care of myself!" Then I say something I never thought I'd have the chance to say. "Grandmother could watch me."

Two little creases appeared between Mom's eyebrows. "And who'd watch Grandmother?"

Flaws or not, I don't think a girl could ever have too many grandmothers. I feel the importance of meeting mine now more than ever. Is my grandmother still mad at Mom for throwing those rocks?

December comes with ice. The sun filters through the leafless trees but isn't nearly warm enough. The nights need blankets.

At school, Amy's job for Jason is to guard the playhouse, and stop any little kids from getting in. I look in on him. He looks like a chained dog. The day before Christmas vacation I free him. I drag him out of the playhouse and into the sunlight. "There, you're free! Wouldn't you rather be free? Jason, you could come dig with me?"

We look at each other and puff the cold air between us.

Then Amy screams for the teacher.
Our punishment is Jason sweeps the play yard, Amy cleans the athletic closet and I sort the math games. Nobody speaks all day.

****

At home that night Dad visits my room looking for the TV remote. I always walk off with it. He finds it on my pillow. "So-wa-da-ya think, Silly Rabbit?"

Mom peeks into my room and puts her hands on her hips. "I haven't told her yet, Steve."

"Told me what?"

"The news, Ivy," Mom teases. "Lou and I have decided we are all going to Cotton Moon for Christmas," Dad says.

"Skoshi, too!" I win! I jump up and down and clap my hands.

I'm nearly too big for Dad to lift me up on his shoulders. His hands make a stirrup for my foot. I hitch up over his big stomach and twist around on his shoulders. He makes a few jumps.

"Yes. You're going to meet your grandmother," Mom says with a tight smile.

That night I dream that I'm standing in court. I must lean way back to see the judge up so high. He looks just like Porky Pig. He wears a long dark robe. He shouts, "It's the last Christmas!" The judge makes that funny stuttering sound. Then he whacks his gavel and shouts

Ghosts of the Canyon

chapter 5

"Wait!" I shout. I scurry to the backyard and scoop up Skoshi's stakeout chain. I grab her food and water bowls. Must haves! Mom and Skoshi are already aboard. I carry on bags stuffed with our Christmas presents. Dad hauls three suitcases at once. As we load up the last of the luggage the phone rings. Dad dashes back into the house as Mom and I get comfortable inside the van.

Dad is back out the front door and gives me his good to go thumbs up sign. "We have LIFT OFF!" He climbs in and starts the van. "Ivy, that was your friend Jason on the phone. He wants me to be sure and tell you…."

I cover my ears and wish I could push out all my anger. "Please, Dad! Give me a break! Don't tell me! I don't want to know! I don't want to hear anything Jason has to say! We are so through! Of all the humiliating, disgusting…"

"Enough, already!" Dad says with the lisp of the Cowardly Lion. "I don't have to take this abuse!"

Mom leans in for the final say. "Knock it off you two! You're scaring the dog."

Dad pushes through traffic, and Skoshi settles down in her dog bed.

Mom talks directions. "Stay in this lane. Keep on the highway." Then later, "Take the next exit." She leans back and relaxes, "for a long time."

I watch the parade passing by my window. A bumper sticker reads, Pray for me. I drive the interstate. That's us! A sign says Stop and Stretch. Another reads, Hail Sale! There are more billboards, and mobile homes and campers.

About an hour north of Fort Worth, the highway narrows to two lanes. Traffic falls away. Concrete disappears. The road turns to blacktop. Then I see a windmill. A barn. Farm equipment dots the fields. Cows munch in pastures and pass us by.

We whiz past small towns. More signs read: Pet Rabbits for Sale, Mutt-Cuts, Dog Grooming, and Hay for Sale.

Mom points. "Those are pecan trees."

Tractors and the biggest rolled bales of hay I've ever seen line the highway. I see a lot of old falling down buildings and houses. More old signs read: Fresh Brown Eggs and Cantaloupe.

Suddenly the sky opens over soft, rolling hills with nothing for sale. "It's all so green," I say.

"scrub oak and cedar," Mom says. "There's been a lot of rain."

The air smells like Christmas, spicy and nutty.

We stop for hamburgers at the Green Lizard Restaurant.

As we enter the restaurant, it's filled with people with chatter floating in the air. A plastic tree sparkles from a table. I shiver and feel that old Christmas tingle: a surprise-waiting, good-things-coming feeling.

"Looks like the whole town's here," I say.

We sit in a green booth with cracked, plastic seats. Ceiling fans hang from a high ceiling. The walls are covered with paintings of horses and cows. High on the wall, right in the big middle of everything, a green lizard, wearing chaps and spurs, rides a bucking horse and waves a ten-gallon hat.

"Halfway there," Dad hands me a Lizard Fry—a fried onion and jalapeno thing. The hamburger patties are made by hand, uneven and crooked. They are cooked with little bits of onion inside and taste sweet.

On our way again out of the parking lot we cross a wooden bridge. In front of us a boy about my age looks up as we pass. He wears a brown-fringed leather jacket, cut-offs, and tennis shoes with no socks.

I turn in my seat to watch him go. I wave.

The boy's face makes a question. He shrugs and looks long. He lifts his arm and waves. Then he fades away in the red haze of our taillights.

"He's wondering who you are," Mom says.

"Everybody's wondering who I am," I say.

We turn onto a two-lane road and go through several small, one-lane towns. In the Metro-plex all the towns touch each other. There's no country in between.

"That's an old, native pecan tree," Dad points. "The small, delicate trees are mesquites."

And that's it for trees. We come onto the flattest land I've ever seen. I point ahead.

"Dad! Is that a lake ahead? It looks like water is splashing on the road!"

Mom and Dad laugh. They say, "It's a mirage—a reflection of the sky."

A pick-up truck passes us. Mom says, "They're not waving yet. Keep watching."

"Who's not waving yet?" I ask.

As we pass through another small town, the radio fuzzes in and out.

"I think one waved," Mom said. "Out here folks wave and wonder who you are and who you're visiting."

The towns get further and further apart.

Along comes a truck. I scoot to the window and wave. "He waved!" I shout.

We all wave back.

Our van cast a long shadow across the fields. The asphalt narrows. The radio makes more fuzz. Then silence.

"I've lost the channel." Dad twists the dials but finds nothing but static.

"What's happening?" I ask. This country leaves me feeling alone.

Our connection, the radio, is gone. We'd been singing Christmas carols with the radio before we stopped for hamburgers. Now, the flavor of
the air changes.

"There is no radio out this far," Mom whispers. "Not until we climb the canyon and come out on the other side. Then we can hear all the stations west of Oklahoma City. Then, we'll be there," she says with a lift in her voice.

Anticipation bites. I feel lost. I'm a long way from home and I don't know what's happening next. I don't know if I'll like Cotton Moon. Or find my brown eyes. What if my cousin is a nerd? It's like on **The Dukes of Hazard** when the car, the Robert E. Lee, is caught in midair and you must wait until after the commercial to see if it makes it or not.

We pass creek beds and hollows where clumps of dry grass sprouts, clinging to patches of red soil. "I see cactus," I say. A wildness seems to be pushing up through the landscape.

We sing "Jingle Bells" and "Sleigh Bells Ring." It's during "We Three Kings" that
I feel the tug of sleep.

I must have dozed off. When I wake it's dark. Mom and Dad talk in low whispers.

"For so long I stayed away. Now, I'm driving right back into it," Mom whispers.

We pass more small towns.

Skoshi needs to walkies," I say.

"Hold on, Skoshi," Dad slows van. "We're coming up on a State Park."

Skoshi whines and wiggles out of my lap.

Gone is the clean green smell. What wafts in the window is dry and dusty. Out the back window, the land is flat. I've never seen sky that comes right down and lies straight against the land. Suddenly a huge scar cuts through the flatness. A canyon has clawed away the land right up to the edge of the road.

"Front and Center! Everybody out! Historical marker!" Dad is a history nut. He thinks it's his duty to rally the family for all historical markers. He moves fast for a stocky guy.

I click on the dog's leash. Skoshi tugs and barks. We find a bush and Skoshi pees. She finds another bush and goes again.

A few minutes later we join Mom and Dad. As we stand silhouetted against Dad's flashlight, he reads: "12,000 years ago pre-historic Indians built alter fires and worshipped in this sacred place. The Spanish explorer, Vasquez de Coronado, stormed through in 1541 looking for gold. In his journal he noted, No gold here, just ghosts that whisper through this cursed, yellow canyon.

Spooked, Coronado rousted his men, and they left before morning.

"Did you know any Indians, Mom?"

"What Indians that were not killed off in the battle of 1876, right across there," Mom points, "were marched off to reservations in Florida."

"Okay….okay." Dad rustles us back into the van.

"Look!" Mom points. "The lights of a city, thirty miles away."

I spy a tiny line of sparkles between the Earth and the sky before we plunge down into the canyon.

My ears pop. I clutch Skoshi when she starts to whine. "There, there, baby." She is such a scared little thing she makes me scared.

Darkness falls quickly. Walls of shadows rise around us. The Sky transforms into a bowl of stars.

"The Big Dipper," Dad points.

The headlights push down into the night. Fear grips me. Ambush! It's like we're heading into an ambush! A ghost screaming bloody war whoops could leap from these dark cliffs and land on top of the van. The headlights pierce the darkness, painting with light splashes of jagged red and yellow rock.

------ As if spooked, like Vasquez de Coronado, Dad eats up the road while Mom and I cling to the blackened windows of the van, eyes wide open for any sign of spirits.

Dad glances back at me and whispers, "This-s-s is-s the tail end of a 35-mile-long canyon made by the wind and water. O-o-o-o-o! Is-s that the wind?"

"Stop it!" I'm already jumpy.

"I don't think it's the wind. It's a ...…Gotcha!"

I think poor Mom nearly chokes. It takes her a minute before she laughs and says, "Quit that, Steve!" She smiles then bites a nail. "The closer we get to Cotton Moon the more nervous I feel. Suddenly, I'm not convinced the past is really over."

"It's over. You've got to believe that." Dad says full of authority. "Your father wants to go on."

"But Daddy doesn't run things," she says anyway. "I'll know when we get there if it's over for Mother and Holly. Or if they're just waiting for an opportunity for revenge."

I try to reassure her. I reach up and touch her shoulder. "We'll be with you, Mom." I wonder how one waits for opportunity.

Grandpa Boots

chapter 6

Standing in the moonlight like a century, a fresh scrubbed, big old house wears a gleaming white coat. It waits for me in the middle of my grandmother's yard. With her trimmed rose bushes all around, the smooth lawn is a smashed-down and withered pale green.

A halo illuminates a holly wreath hanging on the front door. It is strung with walnuts and cranberries and sparkles with little gold angels. A red satin bow dangles from the ceiling.

Dad steps up to the door and bumps right into the mistletoe to ring the doorbell. "Looks like a full-scale, family reconciliation to me."

"Not yet for me." Mom wrinkles her nose at Dad.

I hear the doorbell, a faraway jingle-jangle, coming from inside the house. A door slams. Someone whoops.

Mom snags my hand and whispers, "Here we go. Fasten your seatbelt."

Dad and I meet Mom's daddy as he opens the front door. He peeks around the edge then flings the door wide. He's skinny and wears a red vest and a cowboy string tie. He has singed-looking white hair—a real fuzzed up old man.

He shakes my dad's hand and grins.

Then he turns to me and says, "And you, Ivy Calloway, can give your old Paps a big hug?"

Paps? I hug him to pieces. I feel surprise, his scratchy looking whiskers are soft as feathers.

"Hi, Daddy," Mom says as they hug.

I look past the entrance. I read the words under a framed newspaper picture of my grandpa holding a huge trophy. "For the Craggiest Whiskers in Town." Right there on a table beside the picture sits the trophy with his name on it.

Dad laughs his big laugh at that. "Ha-a!" The berries on the mistletoe shake.

Arm in arm, talking all the way, Mom and my grandpa leads us through an archway into a dark paneled room blazing with candles. Cedar branches drip from a sideboard beside a dining table. Twelve tall mirrors on the left reflect hanging baskets that cover windows on the other side of the room. The room feels like a vine covered cottage with vines on the inside.

In the center, as if made of spun sugar, glistens a tall, lacy tree hanging with gold balls. Tiny lights blink and reflect piles of unopened presents stacked around. And there they are, the unopened presents I'd wished for.

Many clocks fill the room, in niches, on tables, on shelves. Grandpa walks around and talks about his clocks. They all tick together and make a soft whooshing sound. "At midnight they will bong," he says and grins. "Any moment now."

Is it that late?

"Awesome!" I say holding my breath.

First the grandfather clock in the corner starts a low, throbbing moan. Then a shiny black clock with angels all over it tinkles like a bell. A cuckoo clock makes its call. Other birds and bells and gongs and chimes join in stereo from all over the house. Then suddenly all is quiet.

Grandpa's smile covers his face as he watches us as the chorus ends. "First, I set 'em all together," he says. "But they sounded like a freight train."

He then waves his arms at the high ceiling strung with silver garlands. "Granny climbed a ladder to tack those do-dads to the ceiling beams. Every minute I thought she was fixin' to break her neck!" He sprints on and motions for us to follow.

"Joy to the World," sings Dolly Parton from the den TV as we pass by. On a shelf I see a clock with two bronze deer on their hind legs. The antlers almost touch. It's my favorite clock so far. Silver snowflakes decorate the windows in thatroom. In a far corner, narrow stairs hug the wall. I see a fireplace under the stairs.

Skoshi dances in circles around Granpa. She sits back and scratches her ear. "Hush, Skoshi," Mom laughs. "She begs, Daddy, but we don't feed her treats."

Grandpa grins and tosses Skoshi a cashew anyway. "Have a bite, dog." Skoshi jumps up and catches the nut in midair. One swallow and it's gone.

Mom's eyes narrow at Grandpa. I'm pretty sure she's teasing. He shrugs and grins at Mom then winks at me.

I ask, "Who is the little girl in this picture?"

"Well, Ivy Calloway, that's me. Grandpa falls back onto a green velvet couch, breathing hard. Still panting and clutching his chest, he searches frantically through his pockets. He finds and opens a small box and pops a little white pill into his mouth. He continues deep breathing for a while with his eyes closed and his hands resting on his chest. Then he pats the couch beside him.

I sit. I stretch my arm down the velvet armrest. My fingers touch the wood that's carved around the back of the couch.

"Are you okay?" Mom asks, and she throws a searching look at Dad.

Dad moves closer.

Grandpa ignores them both and picks up the picture. "That's me in that picture. Way back then, folks dressed little boy and girl babies the same until they were about three years old way back then in nineteen fourteen. Whoa! That'd make me seventy-nine years old. I'm not that old!" Grandpa slaps his leg and jumps up. "Y'all come on back here." He is still breathing hard.

We follow Grandpa, a little slower this time, straight back through the kitchen to a little glassed-in breakfast porch. The wind blows outside, and the empty branches make scratching sounds on the glass. The room is divided into a breakfast bar with two stools. Grandpa drops onto a bench with pillows and takes a deep breath. I watch his chest go up and down. Dad takes a seat in the wooden rocking chair. We are all warmed by a gas stove. The wood paneling shines. The house smells of spice and holiday magic and has a welcome
all its own.

"Granny's all excited. She has been busy for months getting ready for Christmas," he beams. "She had to hang something in every room. Right now, she is out back in the garden chopping weeds. I'm sure she heard y'all drive up."

I have a grandmother who gardens at midnight?

Glamour Grams

chapter 7

The glass storm door squeaks open.

I turn.

A sweet voice sings out, "Is that my Ivy?"

I smile at the funny hat my granny wears. It's just like the one Mom wears when she works in the yard, a wide brimmed straw hat. That hat pokes in first, and then I notice the eyes, deep brown eyes just like mine. I've found my brown eyes! Or they found me. Those eyes swallow me. My granny is beautiful, a real Glamour Grams. She tosses her garden gloves on an empty chair by the door. She reaches for me, and I melt in her arms.

Glamour Grams is tiny. She's my size. We stand brown eyeball to brown eyeball. She smells of green things from the yard, earthy, clean and full of life.

I claim this grandmother!

"Come see my garden in the moonlight."
Grams tugs at my hand. "Take off your shoes and
socks. The dew has already settled and makes
the grass damp."

"Great." I kick off my shoes and remove
the socks. I step barefooted with my new Grandmother into the night. She takes my hands, and
we twirl round and round on the soft, damp grass.
"We are garden gnomes come to life," I say wild-
ly.

We both giggle. We dance on the lawn under the yard light.

I have the coolest grandmother!

"Look down my rain-barrel," Grams sings.
"Slide down my cellar door, and we'll be jolly
friends for ever more." She twirls me around faster than I twirl her.

"Look at my dinosaur bones in the flower-
beds," she points then bends over and picks up
a rock. "Not exactly bones, I've lined my flower
beds with coprolite. That's just a fancy word for
dinosaur poop! Here, have a hunk!"

She drops a rock thing into my hand.

I make a face.

She fills a bucket with poop shaped rocks.

We laugh so hard we can hardly stand up.

"Thanks, this will really show my friend, Jason." I catch myself. I remember he's not my friend anymore.

The dew drenches my toes. Right then, I breathe in the cool, refreshing midnight air and the cold begins to seep into my bones. I shiver.

Grams puts an arm around me and says, "Let's go inside and make some hot chocolate."

Wow! Grams knows what I want before I do.

As we turn toward the back **porch, I see** a tangle of vines twisting up **the side of the** house. Twining branches climb **up onto the roof.** The tendrils mat together. **A few brown, crum**-bled blossoms droop. If old man winter **hadn't** stopped it, that vine might have covered Grams' house.

But that's not the amazing thing. In the porch light, I see that the plant is still in a coffee can. Or rather, the roots had escaped free of its coffee can prison and found rich soil.

Grams gives my shoulder a squeeze, as she realizes what I'm looking at. "That's Pap's rose! He brought that tacky thing home from one of his old lady friends from the retirement home. He goes down there to play dominoes and chess. They just love him. They act like he's real special." She shakes her head, "I was so mad! It was blooming halfway up the side of the house before I realized I hadn't taken it out of the can. It keeps on blooming just to spite me."

I see her breath in the cool air.

"That's what happens when you don't plant 'em!" Grandpa calls out the back door. His warm, rich voice beckoned like a warm blanket. I want to leap across the lawn to him.

Then looking at Grams, I ask, "Why don't you plant that rose vine, now?"

She turns to me. "Why should I? It's doing so well without me!" Then she laughs out loud, a shrill sound piercing the night air and startling me.

"You know—very well—" Grams shouts back at Grandpa. "That's when I had bronchitis." She prisses up the steps past Grandpa.

"I saved 'em from the plow!" Grandpa winks at Dad. "Used to be, these kinds of roses were planted around the garden gate. Often, they lasted longer than the sod house. The next farmer would come along and plow 'em under. I saved 'em from the plow. Now Lady Banks..."

Grams sniffs and grunts, "I don't want to hear about your old girl friends!"

"Aw, Bell! Come on, Honey! Gi'me a kiss." Grandpa rubs his whiskers against Grams' face.

"You ol' toot!" She says pushing him away, and then says to me, "He's the town character now. Said he had to keep his whiskers just to show Lulu."

"You're just an old woman!" He banters back. Grandpa nudges me as he walks past Grams and whispers, "Hell's Bell!"

What? Is this old-timey cussing? Grandpa is so funny.

Grams prisses on into the living room where Mom waits in the center of the room clinching her arms together.

I hold my breath and watch from the kitchen as Mom and Grams hug. It's stiff and swift. They touch each other then jump back. I'm curious to hear what Grams has to say to my mom after twelve years. Can they be friends now?

They both smile. They see glad to see each other. I hope this will be the end of my mom's sadness. I want this grandmother!

Grams says to Mom in a whisper, "Of course, you do know Steve is fat, don't you?"

It surprises me that Grams is talking about my dad first. He's fat. We already know that. Why does Grams ask Mom if she knows it? I wrinkle my nose in puzzlement.

Mom's shoulders drop and she faintly nods yes. Her eyes become dull. I watch the bright smile slide right off her face.

Is this one of those opportunities Mom was so worried about?

Leaving them alone, I can't find Dad or Grandpa, I explore the house. I count twelve family pictures and my mom isn't in any of them. Grandpa, Grams, Aunt Holly, Uncle Conner, and my two cousins are all dressed up and smiling in each one. Some pictures look down from walls, others look up from tables. They're in and around the clocks and Christmas decorations. A pretty family, but can it be mine if they left my mom out of all the family pictures?

"Lulu is sure lucky to have you, Steve," I hear Grams say sweetly to my dad.

****

Later, as I undress for bed, I overhear Mom and Dad talking.

"You and Daddy went to see Uncle Jake?" Mom shouts in a hoarse whisper. "He was my sister's lawyer!"

"Your dad took me. He was driving. That's where the two bicycles are hidden," Dad explains. "Why didn't you tell me your Uncle Jake was so crippled?"

Friday

chapter 8

Grams whispers, "Santa came early!" She creeps into the den where I sleep and wakes me. Her face is shiny with cold cream and there's a twinkle in her eye.

Two days before Christmas and that old Christmas magic grabs me. I don't know if it's the tree lights dazzling my eyes, the excitement in the air or the smell of pumpkin pies cooking. Two new ten-speed bicycles stand in the living room: one blue and one yellow.

My new cousin, Ernie Gene, waits in the doorway across the room. I suspect he's shy because he avoids my eyes as he quickly bends down on me knee to pet Skoshi.

His soft light hair falls across his eyes. His glasses are thick and heavy and seem to pull his face down. When he looks up again, he pushes them up the bridge of his nose and smiles a quick smile for me. He wears a too big blue and silver band jacket. The room is warm, but he doesn't take it off.

"He walked right over after breakfast." Grams twists her hands then looks at me. "This is your cousin, Ernie Gene."

"I know. Hi." My heart beats. I've got a cousin!

"Hi," he whispers.

Grams reaches out and brushes his collar. "Ernie Gene is so proud of that jacket he never takes it off."

Ernie Gene becomes perfectly still, stiff, like someone is taking his picture. He's almost cringing at her touch.

"He's the shortest boy in high school," Grams says. She hugs him. "This is the smallest size jacket."

Ernie Gene seems to shrink. His shoulders droop. His smile fades and he looks away.

I'm the tallest girl in sixth grade and Ernie Gene only comes up to my ear lobe, but I don't think it would be nice to mention it. That might hurt his feelings. So, why is Grams talking about it?

I hear a knock and Grams opens the front door. "They're here!" She clasps her hands together in joy.

My Aunt Holly comes in first. She is short with dark hair and looks rosy in a Merry Christmas sweater.

"Ivy Calloway, at last!" She wears a big smile and a sprig of plastic holly poked behind one ear. "I'd like to give you a perm. It can be my Christmas present to you." She flicks her fingers through my hair and makes a face.

I look for Mom and Dad to rescue but can find neither.

Uncle Conner follows Holly carrying grocery bags. He's blond, like Michael, and thin and wears a backward baseball cap with a blue flannel shirt. He doesn't look at me but perks up at the sight of my dad and tells him, "I just finished a writing class and am all inspired about Texas landscapes."

They start talking about old windmills and saddles. "There's nothing prettier than an old jail at sunset," Uncle Conner says.

"Good one," Dad says. "Write that down."

Everyone laughs. After a while the conversation gets noisy. Ernie Gene gives me a come on let's go gesture.

"Grab those bikes, Kids!" Grandpa puffs in from the kitchen. He shakes his pocket.

I nab the yellow bike with my name on it.
Ernie Gene takes the blue. He's in a fever to get
away, pushing his bike toward the back door.
Ernie Gene flees, and I quickly follow him on
our new bicycles. We blitz off for parts unknown,
searching out high adventure.

We swing left down Main Street. "That's
my school." Ernie Gene points to a cluster of
brick buildings.

We rocket downhill over a street paved
with bumpy bricks. We bounce all the way to the
courthouse. I stand up on the pedals and shout,
"Look, no hands!" I turn loose of the handlebars,
balance on the seat and reach for the sky. "no feet
either"

I pedal again to catch up with Ernie Gene.
He blazes down an alley behind a row of shops
that face the town square.

"Come this way, Ivy," he says.

A short skid and he parks his bike on the
other side of a gray, cinder brick wall. Half of the
yard side of the wall is painted like a rainbow.
The other half looks like it crashed and flung its
bright colors against a fuzzy-white sky. Old plastic chairs grey

with age, overturned tables and piles of stomped
on beer cans litter the weed-infested yard. I see
a dirty, red plaid shirt thrown over a chair and an
emptied-out but well used as tray.

We creep up to the back of the decayed
building. Mom already told me that the front is a
beauty shop for Aunt Holly and a clock shop for
Grandpa. An upstairs apartment is shared by my
aunt and uncle and cousin.

Ernie Gene and I sprint over withered
plants in pots sitting on top of rusted, twisted
metal things. I spy a miniature windmill captured
by a twining vine.

"That's Mom's art," Ernie Gene says. "She
does metal sculptures."

There's art everywhere in the yard. What a
mess! I'd hate to live here.

"What happened? Is this a left-over party?" I could only guess.

"Not 'til Thursday, Mom's day off." Ernie
Gene kicks a can crusher aside so we could get up

the steps to the back door. "It's always like this,"
he says.

We enter a dark musty hall.

His room has no window and looks like a
pantry. A dirty cracked linoleum floor with ratty
dirt encrusted braided rugs are flung around. A
banged-up bureau and a dresser has a hideously
dark mirror.

We must back out as he reaches up and pulls
down a squeaky metal bed. The bedspread is a
nappy, blue and silver blanket. His sheets are
gray, and the pillow is flat.

He points to the blanket. "School colors,"
he mutters proudly.

From under the ragged mattress, he pulls a
rolled up brown paper sack. "Firecrackers! Spar-
klers! I've saved them!" He holds them out to me
like some kind of pirate's treasure. A slow grin
tugs at the corners of his mouth.

Slam!!!

We jump as a door slams and angry voices
rise from the front of the building. It sounds like
Aunt Holly and Uncle Conner are screaming and

cussing. Ernie Gene's face turns white. All expression drains. His shoulders tighten.

"They're back! Let's get out of here!"
He shoves the fireworks into his jacket pocket.
I catch his fear. We vamos out the back door,
snatch our bikes and go.

Ernie Gene peddles ahead, and I follow.
He looks back once, and then lowers his head and
speeds faster. He stops at the end of the alley that
 faces the highway.

"Leave the bicycles here." Ernie Gene
props his blue one against the wall.

He finds a hammered together door I hadn't
seen before and opens it for me.

A Bully for Ernie Gene

chapter 9

As Ernie Gene opens the door, I enter and
light darts inside the shadowy interior of the
Cotton Moon Club. The room blazes to light then
returns to shadows and eerie silence when I shut
the door behind us.

I hear a pinball machine ringing and
whizzing from a dim corner. A bunch of Cotton
Moon's tough-looking guys lean heavily on the
only pinball machine in the place. Others watch
the player as he laughs and shakes the machine.
A hunk of grungy hair falls over his eyes. He
scratches his poochy belly through a hole in his
tee shirt and ignores us as we enter.

I trail behind Ernie Gene, as he ventures
forward. I'm not sure about this. I can still run for
it! But no, I wouldn't do that to Ernie Gene.

My cousin is already standing beside the
counter and has ordered sodas, chips and jerky. I
climb onto a round stool beside him feeling the
coldness of the room through the cracked
plastic seat.

A girl laughs. Her shrill screech pierces the
air. A moment later I focus my eyes on a dripping

candle that'd been stuck in an empty bottle of
wine.

The girl sits there with three whispering,
laughing teen girls, at a table covered with a red
and white checkered tablecloth

"Move it, Williams!" Mr. Hole-y Tee Shirt
punches the arm of the taller boy standing next to
him.

"Ow!" Skinny Williams scowls an angry
face.

Hole-y Tee Shirt tries to grab his sore arm,
but Williams sidles away.

Then, Hole-y Tee Shirt shoves his way
across the room.

Ernie Gene is talking to a girl behind the
counter. I'll bet she's a real beauty under her
make-up. She's probably in high school. This
place must be the high school hangout. It looks
like an explosion in a Pizza place, then a bunch of
PTA mothers came in and...

"Hey, Arm Rest!" Hole-y Tee Shirt is suddenly next to us and rams his big elbow on top
of Ernie Gene's head. "I'm talking to you, Arm
Rest!" Then he folds his other arm and jabs that
elbow on top of Ernie Gene's head.

Startled, I nearly fall off my stool.

The girls at the table giggle and cover their mouths with their hands.

Williams adds his elbow to the top of Ernie Gene's head. "Yeah, we're talking to you, Arm Rest!"

I kneel to pick up Ernie Gene's glasses and he sort of falls on me. Irritated with Williams, Hole-y Tee Shirt pokes him in the neck with his elbow.

"Ow!" Williams slaps Hole-y Tee's ear. "Leave me alone!"

Forgetting about Ernie Gene, Hole-y Tee grabs Williams' arm and twists it behind his back "Oh, yeah?"

"Enough of you two! You've been warned about this before. Now get out!" Pretty Girl behind the counter frowns and points to the door.

Both boys make angry looks at her, but they leave.

When they're gone, she says to us, "Don't worry about them, Ernie Gene. They won't be back today.

Ernie Gene and I finish our drinks then he says, "We better go, too."

"I agree. Grams might worry, right?" I slide off the stool and head for the door.

"Wha . . .? Ernie Gene looked confused. "Who'd worry?"

My brow furors in question.

"Oh, you mean Granny," he says. "You call her Grams? Then what do you call Paps?"

"You mean Grandpa. When we first got here last night, Grandpa said I could give my old Paps a hug. I didn't know what he meant."

"You call him Grandpa?"

"Yeah!"

Ernie Gene shrugs his shoulders.

As we leave the Cotton Moon Club, Ernie Gene waves and everybody waves back. I wave, but no one waves back. The girls still gape at me with big eyes and mouths wide open. Strangers must be scarce here. They don't see many city folk. Or is it that I'm with Ernie Gene?

What a bunch of zombies!

Outside the sun beams and gives me tears. Then I see mad! Hole-y Tee has Ernie Gene's bike and is ready for take-off! Williams and Hole-y Tee are stealing our bikes!

I scatter dirt and gravel as I spring into the alley. "Get off! You're not stealing this bike!" I shout into Hole-y Tee's shocked face. I jerk hard on the handlebars.

I don't think Ernie Gene is much of a fighter and he hangs back. I don't want a fight, but it looks like there might be one. And I am going to be right in the big middle of it because I'm not letting go of this bike. Between the bully and me the bike doesn't budge. I don't turn loose.

Hole-y Tee settles down on the seat. "Who are you?" He smirks.

Williams eases up beside me. "Yeah! Who are you?" He removes his sunglasses and slips them into the pocket of his blue and silver band jacket, a jacket just like Ernie Gene's.

Two sets of eyes bare that question down into me. Who am I? I don't know. I know my name, of course, but I don't really know who I am.

I have Grams' brown eyes; will I become like her when I grow up? I live with my mom; will I be like her? How about Old Dad? How much of him will I have? Who am I? I think about the question. I come back to reality as two huge high school boys full of anger glare at me.

Ernie Gene wanders up beside me. "She's my cousin," he remarks.

Williams jerks and steps back. "Hey man, we didn't know!"

Now I realize who I am! I'm Ernie Gene's cousin. I like the sound of that. The Cotton Moon Club made me a stranger; Ernie Gene makes me family. I didn't know until that moment just how really smart my cousin is.

Hole-y Tee slides off the seat and hands the bike to Ernie Gene. "Yeah, Arm Rest! We didn't know she was your cousin." His elbow makes a stab at Ernie Gene's head but misses. Then Ernie Gene jumps out of there leaving two astonished boys.

I grab my bike. We peddle like mad! Suddenly, we are my favorite TV show, **The Dukes of Hazard** on the back roads of town.

I'm their girl cousin up from the big city. We're running from the long arm of the law.

Then I see Boss Hogg. He eases up behind us in his black and white and parks. A gold star gleams from the side of his car, The Cotton Moon Sheriff.

Ernie Gene sees him, too. "Hey, watch this," he whispers. He pulls something from his pocket and throws it in the street, and then he turns around and tears back into the alley.

I follow fast as I can, not knowing why. Then I know why. And I am glad I am quick.

Pop! Pow! Kaboom! Ernie Gene is throwing lit firecrackers! He throws them up left and right as he peddles his bike down the alley. Most of them pop in the air. Some make wonderful colors. Others make clouds that burst into sparkles. The alley lights up like a carnival in full swing!

I pump up beside him and look over. Ernie Gene's face tells me nothing. He watches mine instead. Like he wants to see what my face is doing.

My eyes are bulging. My face is both shrieking and oo-o-ing and aa-a-ing. Ernie Gene seems to see the emotions I feel, wonder and surprise with a little fear. His expression stays perfectly still leaving me wondering why. Are all his feelings inside?

As soon as I can breathe, I shout, "What are you doing? That cop will come and get us!"

Ernie Gene stops his bike, turns and points. "No. He's not chasing us. He knows who I am. And now he knows who you are, too."

I wonder at this. How could he know that?

I look at the sheriff at the other end of the alley as he stretches, yawns and calmly checks his tires.

Ernie Gene gathers his bike and turns toward the house. "This morning my mother decided my job was to clean up the beer cans in our back yard, but I ran over to Granny's to meet you instead and we got our bikes. You remember?"

"This morning?" A long time ago. Ernie Gene's been in a rush to be gone ever since.

He nods his head and pushes off into Main Street.

I follow and catch up.

"I would've got a knuckle rack from Paps for sure this morning." he says. Ernie Gene pops his knuckles against his head loud enough for me to hear. "By now he's forgotten."

I puzzle at this: Is my cousin afraid of Grandpa? I can't imagine fearing Grandpa, or of him hurting Ernie Gene. More doubts chew at me. It's too awful to think about.

"What about those two guys back there?" I ask.

Ernie Gene snorts. "They're only bullies. They're in my class at school. Anyway, I'm used to it," he says. He pushes his glasses up and looks away.

I don't get it. Have we been hiding from Grandpa? Did my cousin take me to The Cotton Moon Club to hang-out with a couple of bullies so he wouldn't get a knuckle rack from Grandpa?

Party Time

chapter 10

My cousin and I peddle quickly back to the house. We park the bikes by some overgrown lilac bushes. Then we march in the back door.

Grandpa is playing his old country music records. He's holding the thin, round black record by the tips of his fingers. He touches only the edges. Then he places it on the spinning base and slowly lowers an arm with a needle. As soon as it makes contact, cowboy guitar music bounces off the rafters.

"Turn it down!" Grams says.

All my new relatives are here. They have taken up seats around the kitchen: Grandpa in the love seat by the fire looking up at Mom, Mom beside him on a stool looking down at him. Grams beside Mom on a stool talking to Holly, who walks all over the kitchen. Dad and Uncle Conner laugh at something. They're all talking at once.

I feel glad. Things are turning out just like I want them to. It's a grand family reunion indeed. Even more unopened presents have been stacked around the Christmas tree.

The back of Aunt Holly's red sweater reads: "A Reindeer ran over Grandma!" I wonder if Aunt Holly is thinking of Grams.

Grandpa squints his eyes at me and Ernie Gene. "Where have you two been?"

I can't pick up his mood from his voice. So, I don't know if he's teasing or not.

"You were supposed to be home an hour ago." Grandpa has an even harder look for Ernie Gene.

"Are you ready for this story or not, Paps?" All eyes turn to Uncle Conner.

Grandpa turns away and laughs with Uncle Conner. My uncle begins to tell a story but gets nowhere because everyone talks at once. They're grown-ups interrupting each other like kids.

Uncle Conner begins, again. "My Most Special Place in a castle high in the mountains of Mexico." He stretches his long arms to form them. "A Holiday Inn bought it. This place had incredible sunsets and the most sparkling springs. I took Holly there for our honeymoon, thinking she would love it as much as I did." Uncle Conner busts out laughing. He pulls a handkerchief from his jeans and wipes his eyes. "We rode little donkeys up and down these picturesque mountain trails with wildflowers everywhere. Holly had

temper fits and beat the poor, little donkeys!"
He howls again. Everybody roars. Uncle Conner
struggles to continue. "Finally, at dinner, she was
so rude to the waiters they refused to serve her!
They scattered whenever they saw her coming.
They named her "La Gringa!" Everyone laughs
even louder

Uncle Conner blows his nose. Grandpa
slaps his knee. Grams shakes her curls and dabs
her eyes with a Christmas napkin. And I don't
get it. Then I hear Dad's big laugh. If something
strikes him funny, he lets out a yell. It's a little
like Ha-a! But more of a howl. It's loud and
makes other people laugh, too. When I hear it, my
whole world is right. Dad laughs so I laugh, too.

I spot Ernie Gene waving me back into the
kitchen, but Grandpa catches me by my arm as I
walk past. He grins like a kid. He hugs me tight.
He tickles me with his short whiskers. "Glad
you're here, Ivy," he whispers. He croons along
with his old records, "Deep in my heart there's a
melody . . ." then something about old San Anto-
nio before I could wiggle away.

In the kitchen Ernie Gene says "It's my birthday. Help me carry in presents."

"Your birthday? What a surprise! Is this the party?"

He loads me up to the chin with presents. Grams comes in and lights the candles on his cake. He follows her into the dining room singing Happy Birthday.

Grams says, "My Holly's birthday is on Christmas day, so we never have a party for her. It's too close to Christmas and Christmas always won out. Ernie Gene's birthday is two days before, so it's far enough away from Christmas to have a party."

How sad to think Aunt Holly never having a birthday party.

Ernie Gene and his stepdad Conner are on hands and knees struggling with the new Spindle Game we gave him. Uncle Conner holds a short straw with his thumb and finger to steady it.

I coach, because I've done this before, "Put the straw through the top of the spindle and blow really hard," I tell them.

Everybody watches and cheers as the two tops whirl in a little arena. Ernie Gene's pops off Uncle Conner's first. We all cheer for Ernie Gene.

"You picked a good game, Lou," Aunt Holly says to my mom.

Grams sits a steaming pot on the table. Uncle Conner has made crab gumbo. That's potato soup with little bites of crab meat in it. It's late by the time we eat.

Dad gets the "Killer Chair"—the one that wobbles and nearly falls apart when anyone sits on it. It brakes with him, cracking as it falls. Dad lands on his bottom and bounces a few times. He sits there and clutches his bowl of gumbo. Not a drop spilt. "Ha-a!"

Everyone cheers.

After supper Grandpa brings out another stack of his old country records, and despite many groans of protest, he carefully plays each one. He

doesn't care. He pats his foot and loses himself in
"Jodi Blonde."

Later Grandpa teases my dog. Skoshi chas-
es a flashlight beam across the floor. We all laugh
and call her the "battery operated dog."

The more the adults talk the louder they
get. There's conversation about what everybody
is drinking. Grandpa is drinking one kind of beer.
Grams and Aunt Holly like a different beer and
they argue with him about which one is best.

My cousin motions come here. I take my
lead from Ernie Gene. He knows all the hiding
places. We stay out of sight, hidden behind the
grown-up's party. That's easy. Grams and Grandpa, or even his own parents, hardly ever look at
Ernie Gene. He acts like if Grandpa notices him,
he'll remember that knuckle rack. It seems he
tries to be invisible, and when I'm with him, I try,
too.

We skirt the edge of the party and plan as-
saults on fruitcake and ham as needed for our hiding place. My new cousin and I sit cross-legged
in a corner of the hall floor. Our small triangle

room creates itself as the kitchen door opens and folds back over the den door. The two doorknobs overlap. We're hidden along with the water heater and the vacuum cleaner. We hear everything going on in the kitchen.

****

"I'm sorry . . . I'm sorry . . ."
Aunt Holly says "I'm sorry" like breathing out and breathing in. It's before and after everything she says, like a spastic hiccup, filling all the empty spaces. "Does Ivy still visit her father?" She asks
"Oh, yes. Ivy does visit," Mom says. "They're alcoholics. So, I'm not keen on long visits."

****

Inside our hiding place, Ernie Gene's hands twitch along the door facing. "Don't jiggle the doorknobs together. Nobody has discovered this hiding place."
I didn't know Ernie Gene very well. I usually asked him a lot of questions. But I didn't ask why he needed hiding places.

93

As we watch through one hinge of our triangle room, we see our mothers sitting together at the kitchen bar. Through the other hinge we could see Skoshi asleep on the couch. I smell the popcorn Grandpa is popping.

"I miss my dad." Ernie Gene leans closer to me. "I don't see him much."

"You mean your Old Dad?"

"No," Ernie Gene's eyes pierced mine. "I don't. I mean my real dad who lives in Fort Worth with my brother Sam."

"I get it!" I say. "Your real dad and Steve, my New Dad, treat us special. You must like it here about as much as I like it at my Old Dad's."

"Yes, when I go visit my dad, I'm special." Ernie Gene sits with his empty bowl on the floor. "We talk and do movies together and play golf and soccer. Sam's the best big brother a guy could have!" Ernie Gene's mouth falls in a soft curve. His eyes dream. "I haven't seen him in a couple of years."

The Hiding Place

chapter 11

From the safety of our hiding place, I see Aunt Holly stand up defiantly. "But, Louise, we're alcoholics!" Then her face softens, and she says, "I'm sorry . . I'm sorry" to Grams and Uncle Conner . . . She lowers her chin and backs away from Mom. Aunt Holly makes a funny look at Grams, and then glares at Mom with her chin up, a what-are-you-going-to-do-about-it look on her face.

Grandpa turns and flashes Mom a smile "Drink up, Lulu. To be with us, you have to be an alcoholic."

On the kitchen cabinet they slosh brown whiskey around in bottles as big as milk gallons. Grandpa Boots pours Mom's whiskey into an iced tea glass.

I muffle a giggle as I remember mom saying she only likes the drinks that come with little umbrellas.

Back in Fort Worth Old Dad keeps his booze bottles put away. He and Mary, his wife, go out to bars to drink. When they come home, her kids run and hide or climb out the back bedroom windows before Old Dad starts throwing furniture. I was little then and did not know. I was nearly nicked by a flying chair.

Was furniture going to fly here?

****

"I had to become an alcoholic to be with my children." Grams moans and her eyes find Aunt Holly's across the breakfast bar.

"I'm sorry . . . I'm sorry . . ." Aunt Holly whines. She pats Grams' hands.

They all jump when Dad cruises into the kitchen and stabs the last of the sausage balls. "What's going on in here?" He beams.

Aunt Holly turns and tosses him her very best smile, "Louise is sure lucky to have you, Steve," she warbles.

****

At bedtime Skoshi and I sit on the den couch, snuggling in Grams' quilt. Ernie Gene watches us with his solemn face. His glasses reflect the blinking lights of the Christmas tree. His pillow and pallet wait on the floor beside me.

"Hot chocolate," Grams sings. She sits down a tray with a bowl of popcorn and three cups overflowing with marshmallows.

Grams tells us the story of her Christmas baby—Aunt Holly. "She was born on Christmas morning with long dark curls. Looking like an angel. The nuns in the hospital came to kneel and pray. That's pretty holy, and us Protestants and all."

Tiny rain drops begin to fall. I sure wish it would snow.

Grams kisses the three of us good night. Even Skoshi.

The Crazy Stuff

chapter 12

In my nightmare a woman is screaming. She yells in some foreign language. I can't understand what she's saying. I try to wake up. No longer asleep in the crook of my elbow, Skoshi tenses, her ears twitch. A low growl rises in her throat.

A sharp bark escapes her throat, and my entire body flinches. Torn from sleep, I want to sit up but can't. I stare into the darkness. My eyes search for what woke me. Skoshi presses herself against me, and a soft growl once more rumbles in her chest. Then, stroking her fur I silence her growl, and hear something else.

"Dirty LIAR!"

My heart begins to race. My hands tighten on my little dog, and I feel her muscles stiffen.

"What is it?" I whisper to her.

Skoshi wriggles loose from my grasp and jumps off the bed. She disappears into the darkness. The voices I heard had vanished, and all I can hear now is Skoshi snuffling along the far wall, sniffing along the baseboard and under the door.

"Skoshi?" I whisper again. "What is it, Baby?"

My dog runs back to the bed, leaps onto it, and licks my face. I pull her closer, snuggling her against my body the way I did my teddy bear when I was little. I feel Skoshi's heart beating and the warmth of her body. She whimpers and I take comfort.

From the dining room, the nightmare woman yells words I cannot understand. She makes spitting and hissing sounds; "Of course you do know I love you, Louise."

I hear my mom's voice. "You don't act like you do, Sister."

"Because you're a dirty Liar! Liar!" The screamer screams.

"We love you, Lulu," Grams says. "It's you who can't feel our love."

Grams is in my nightmare? Did I fall asleep again?

"You're just selfish! You lie!"

"Are we're playing that old game?" Mom asks.

They are playing a game. The Game of Love?

Suddenly, I am back in school, in the oak tree with Teha, our legs dangling. The leaves sing as the wind breathes. I love you a bushel and a peck!

Then I'm back to my nightmare. The nightmare woman screams some more. I must be asleep. I hover between Teah in our tree and the nightmare screams. I can almost open my eyes. They flutter and twitch, turning my blackness into a symphony of flashing colors.

"Dirty LIAR!"

"*. . . a bushel and a peck. . .*"

It doesn't sound like a game. I rub my eyes, feeling more and more confused.

"Dirty LIAR!"
"*. . .a bushel and a peck. . .*"

"Dirty LIAR!" The hysterical voice is coming from Grams' kitchen.
"*. . . a bushel and a peck and a hug around the neck!*"

With a pinch in my stomach, I try to remember where I am. But something is wrong. Am I in Grams' house or in a nightmare?

I open my eyes and I can see the hall lit from the kitchen light. The dining room door is closed, and my corner of the den is dark.

"You are a dirty LIAR!"

"Holly, you already said that." My mom's voice tugs me more awake.

Prickles crawl up my spine. I pull the covers around me and my dog. With Skoshi beside me the room doesn't seem so dark.

"Dirty LIAR!"

I can't believe it. The voice is Aunt Holly's!

Are Mom and her sister playing their game of love?

I gag at a copper taste in the back of my mouth. I can't swallow. I'm not sure I can breathe.

Is someone going to hurt my mom?

"Why are you continuing on with this?" My mom's voice is louder.

"Of course, you know why!" That's Grams.

Aunt Holly shrieks even louder. "YOU'RE A FILTHY LIAR!"

"You're not rational . . ." my mom begins.

"What do you want?" Aunt Holly screams. "WHY DID YOU COME HERE?"

Mom says, "I came to see Daddy."

"That's obvious!" Grams snorts.

"YOU FILTHY . . .!"

"He asked me here," Mom goes on, "But I wouldn't be here if I thought you two weren't through with this stuff. I hoped it would be different this time. Daddy's sick. I thought . . ."

"You thought . . . You thought," mocks Grams.

"And you, Mother, why didn't you tell my birthing story? You know the one. The nurse brings me in, and you laugh at your bald, wrinkled little monkey baby. You laughed so loud the nurse took me away. "

"You can't feel love, Lulu," Grams says again.

"Dirty LIAR!"

Why are they yelling at my mom? I feel groggy. Then I close my eyes, I feel like I still pedaled my bike. But I can't pedal away from Aunt Holly's screams.

"Dirty LIAR!"

My head stays glued to the pillow. I don't want to get up anymore. A chill flows through my veins and makes my fingers ice cold.

"YOU TWO-FACED LIAR!"

The Christmas tree no longer twinkles. Black shadows fill the room. Darker thoughts fill my head.

When did the Christmas music stop . . .?

"Dirty LIAR!"

. . . And this crazy stuff began?

"STU-PID LIAR!"

I've never done or said anything that made people this mad. At least Ernie Gene still sleeps tight on his pallet beside my couch. I hear his steady breathing. Can he be faking it?

"Dirty LIAR!"

Where's my dad? He'll put a stop to this!

I throw the covers back, swing my legs off the couch, and stand up. My heart makes a hollow racket. I plop back down. My breath comes short. Am I having a heart attack?

"YOU DIRTY. . .!"

Mom interrupts, "You're repeating your-self, now, Holly."

Way to go, Mom!

Aunt Holly wails, "Dirty LIAR!" She gets louder and louder. That's when she blows. It sounds like she's raging around the dining room, kicking chairs and getting louder still.

I can't see anything but the darkened room I'm trapped in. I hear bumps and moving furni-ture. I can do nothing but shiver and hug the quilt around me and my quivering dog.

My gut clenches with dread.

How can I be trembling just hearing what-ever this is? And why? How could Grams let Aunt Holly shriek at my mom?

"Dirty LIAR!"

Aunt Holly and Grams hate Mom? Is this about hate? Is this about throwing rocks? Were we invited here for their revenge? Or is this the way Cotton Moon does Christmas?

I must get up, but I'm too scared and tired.

I put my head under my pillow. The clocks bong four o'clock. Each bell sends a curling tendril down through a dark cave looking for me. If I keep still and my eyes tight shut, they can't find me. But, with nudges and pokes from those tendrils, the bongs of the clocks swirl about my ears with bright flashes.

I open my eyes when Skoshi whines and noses open the door to the dining room. The door stays open a few inches, and I can see light from the other room. A beam like a flashlight falls across us. The dog hops up and licks my fingers then burrows under the covers.

I lean over a bit. I can see Mom and Aunt Holly through the cracked door. Is this still going on? Mom stands in the dining room with her back to me. My aunt sits on a stool.

I throw off the covers and creep over Ernie Gene. I toe silently to the cracked door for a better look. Grams sits at the table rocking back and forth. She's crying. She makes a fist and beats it on the table. She flexes her fingers. Then she clutches her hands together again. Her pixie face, last night so full of love, is now ugly, mean and twisted. Her eyes are red and puffy.

I think for a second that she has spotted me. She twitches a crooked smile in my direction, but Grams can never take back that look of rage and hatred I saw on her face. I will never forget it as long as I live. Everything has changed between us forever.

I jump back to Skoshi and the covers when Aunt Holly starts screaming again. Then she stops and sobs. Again, Aunt Holly makes spitting and hissing sounds.

I curl into a tight ball, my toes cold. I stuff the covers up around my neck. Clutching a whining Skoshi to my stomach, we watch as my new grandmother turns into a nightmare.

I don't think I want to claim this grandmother anymore.

We stay still and watch Aunt Holly through the cracked door. She jerks her arms. Her clenched fists wrestle the air. She cries out loud then the air bursts out of her like a balloon. "I'm sorry . . . I'm sorry." She quivers up at Uncle Conner who suddenly stands behind her.

I feel a stab in my stomach.

Uncle Conner hates my mom, too?

He rubs Aunt Holly's shoulders. He leans over and makes soft sounds in her ear.

Why is Uncle Conner comforting Aunt Holly? She is nuts-o!

"Holly's out of control . . ." Mom echoes my thoughts

"Dirty LIAR!"

" . . . And needs to get herself a therapist"

Aunt Holly weeps louder. "I'm sorry," she says.

". . .Or an exorcist!" Mom finishes then says, "Yes, you are sorry, Holly."

Wow! Did my mom tell them or what?

My grandmother jumps up and speeds across the room. She throws her arms around Aunt Holly. "This is a fine woman, Louise!"

She and Uncle Conner bunch up behind my aunt. They pose like an old-fashioned valentine card, all making soft cooing sounds at Aunt Holly.

My mom stands all alone on the other side of the room.

"She's sick, Mother!" Mom's almost shouting. "I thought y'all were through with this narcissistic name-calling stuff and wanted to be a family. I've heard enough. I won't come back."

How much more of this can I take? My head throbs. My stomach hurts. I need a drink of water bad.

Mom seems to wait a long time before she says, "It's your loss and I'm sad for you."

From the other side of the dining room, comes a choked response from Aunt Holly. "So why don't you just commit suicide?"

A look of grim satisfaction spreads across my grandmother's face. She nods and cries, "Oh . . . yes . . . .do! Do!" A wild glee takes hold of her. Her hands flap like captured birds. She smashes them and mashes them. She fights them and they get away and she catches them again.

Commit suicide?

The words exploded inside my head like Grandpa's popcorn against the sides of the hot pan.

Grandmother and Aunt Holly demand my mom commit suicide? Even if she didn't want to? Would they help her a little? I'm terrified they would, and I'd be helpless to stop it.

The Old Walrus

chapter 13

I must have slept, then I suddenly jerk from a deep nothing. What woke me? The house is still but for the whisper of ticking clocks.

A huge moon reflects off the light rain and spreads a glow across the den. I so want my first white Christmas, then I remember my grandmother.

I look across the darkened den and see Grandpa slouching in a wheelchair. No one told me he was sick enough to need a wheelchair! I don't know who to be mad at. Someone should have told me.

He seems to be gazing at the quiet, empty kitchen. The stage is dark.

He breathes a while into a machine that sounds like Darth Vader. I think it's an oxygen bottle. Then he sobs into his sleeve, stifling the sound. He does that over and over again.

It must have been his sobbing that woke me. The coldness begins to come again. I want to go put my arms around him. I move my feet to get up. Then I think he might feel embarrassed if he knew I was watching, so I lay very still.

My two deer are forever leaping across the white face of a clock.

I slowly turn my head toward the ceiling. A swell of sadness engulfs me. A tear slides out the corner of my eye and loses itself in my ear. It's warm and wet.

Am I in the Twilight Zone, in a family full of Zombies? The clocks chime five thirty. I fall asleep listening to Grandpa breathe and sob with his whispering clocks.

****

I dream. I'm swimming and look up through murky, green water. I see an old walrus sitting on the dock crying. He wipes his eyes with a little handkerchief that isn't nearly big enough for the tears he's shedding.

When I wake, it's morning. I think the dream is over. But the old walrus keeps on crying.

"Ernie Gene?" I whisper and reach down to his pallet. My hand touches the carpet. My cousin is gone, his blanket, his knapsack, gone.

Was he kidnapped? Snatched in his sleep? Dragged out of here in the middle of the night?

Fear rises in my throat like vomit, and I wondered if this grandmother thing is a really bad idea.

"What's wrong, Daddy?" Mom asks from the kitchen.

The old walrus stops crying.

"Bell said y'all are leaving this morning and Christmas is cancelled."

Forever

chapter 14

Christmas Eve morning and my eyes won't open.   Is it still Christmas Eve when Christmas is cancelled? I'd have to ask Grandpa that one.

From my safe place under the covers with Skoshi, I hear Mom ask my grandmother in the kitchen, "Were you trying to kill him? We came for Christmas. Christmas is not cancelled and we're not leaving." Mom said softer, "Don't hurt him, Mother. I get your point. We won't ever come back."

I don't hear what she says to that. But I hear her on the kitchen phone a few minutes later. "No . . . no . . .I'm all right, Holly. I can handle that . . .no . . .no . . Tell him Louise hasn't tried anything . . .yet."

What does my grandmother think my mom will do?

I watch my grandmother wander through the den a couple of times, not focusing her eyes properly. Her lips moving but no words come out.

I want to ask her, "Don't you remember me? I'm the kid whose Christmas you just can-celled!"

But Grandmother acts like I'm not here, or not important enough.

I feel really down and worried. "Is Grandpa all right?" I ask her.

Grandmother spies me. Her eyes widened. So wide I can see her bloodshot whites all around her deep brown eyes. My brown eyes! Would I grow up to be like her?

She acts like she just saw me for the first time. "He's fine," she says then starts giggling, "Tee, he, he, he, he." Grandmother covers her mouth with a handkerchief and dashes into the kitchen.

What's wrong with her? I want to tell her it's just me—only a kid. Suddenly I feel trapped in a room I cannot stand another minute.

I dress in a flash and find Mom in the front bedroom drinking coffee in bed.

"You look awful," I tell her.

She gives me a crooked smile. "You should see the other guy."

Dad is already dressed. "Slept great," he says and kisses Mom bye. He leaves and must have found Grandpa. I hear them slam out the back door.

"Ernie Gene's gone!" I cry to Mom and curl up on her covers so she would rub my back.

Mom rubs her own head instead. "His parents came and took him."

"What-a-a-t?"

"They said I was dangerous," Mom says. "Go find me an aspirin, will you, Ivy?"

Mom dangerous? Has everybody gone nuts?

I search around the bathroom but don't know where the aspirin is. I must ask my grandmother. She brings Mom the bottle and a glass of water.

"Poor Lulu doesn't feel well," Grandmother says to no one in particular.

Mom takes the aspirin but doesn't smile back at Grandmother. Instead, she gives me her "how could you?" look. She seems irritated because I had brought my grandmother.

As gloom settles over the place, I wander into the living room. I cannot wait to bike over to Ernie Gene's to find out what happened last night. No one around here is talking.

Out the windows I see Aunt Holly drive by the side of the house and park in the back.

About that same time, I hear Ernie Gene slam his bike down out front. He whizzes in. He had come for me, so together we start toward the door.

"Watch out for the bullies," my grandmother hisses after us, drawing us back, urgently.

We turn around to be polite.

Ernie Gene nods at my grandmother, "Yes ma'am."

I shoot a look back through the house. I can see through the dining room, through the kitchen, and out the back porch. Aunt Holly is hauling grocery sacks in.

"Don't worry," I look back at my grandmother. "If they bother us, I can talk to them. I'm good at that."

I hear Aunt Holly plop her grocery sacks in the kitchen. She heads toward us.

I think Ernie Gene is fixin' to pop right out of his britches. He twitches this way and that, making let's go gestures.

Grandmother's hands touch Ernie Gene's face, his hair, then rest on his shoulder. She runs a finger down his jaw, lifting his chin. Like she'd snagged him with one finger. He might as well be caught by a fishhook.

Ernie Gene stands as still as stone. He doesn't breathe. Not an eyelash moves. At his neck, a blue vein throbs.

"Oh, that's right." My grandmother drops her hands and wipes them on her yellow Ask Granny apron. She slides a look at Mom, who is mumbling to herself and practically shoving us out the door. Grandmother seems to be enjoying herself. She turns with a twirl and sings to Aunt Holly, "Ivy's parents have taught her to love the little brats."

Mom gasps.

I reach over and put my arm around her. I say the nicest thing I can think of. "There's not a mean bone in my mom's body."

My grandmother makes a sideways sniff and peers over her glasses at Aunt Holly, who rolls her tongue around inside her cheek like she has a marble.

My grandmother turns loose of Ernie Gene,
he skid addles out the door, with a hold of me.

The icy wind feels good on my face.

"Is it always like this around here?" I ask
Ernie Gene as we peddle away.

"Like what?"

****

The downtown barber shop next door to
Grandpa's Clock Shop has a Nativity scene in the
window. An aluminum star hangs crooked. The
three wise men are Popsicle sticks. Glued cotton
ball farm animals kneel before a tiny, plastic Jesus. Wrapped in tinsel, the babe sleeps in a
matchstick manger.

Nobody can cancel Christmas!

Ernie Gene and I walk into Grandpa's
Clock Shop. He perches high on a wooden stool,
stooping over a tall table. He looks like an elf, or
a funny bird, or an acrobat all twisted up. Where
is his wheelchair? Will he need his oxygen bottle?
I can find no part of the sick man I heard crying
in the night.

Behind him stretches a wall of paperback westerns. Grandpa nods back over his shoulder. "I've read every one of those, Steve. The one you've got there in your hand is my favorite."

My dad thumbs through "The Riders of the Purple Sage".

I can hear Aunt Holly rattling around in her beauty shop next door. That's where I will be getting my permanent later today. Oh my God!

My stomach jumps. Hope she doesn't fry my hair.

Behind the library wall, the two shops become one long room of junk.

Ernie Gene scrams on through to his room.

I look up at Grandpa. "What a cool table."

"I searched all over for this." He says. "Couldn't find the one I wanted so I make it myself!" He turns his face to me. He scrunches his eyebrow and wraps his eyelid around this black looking glass thing. He squints through it like Popeye.

"Come take a look."

To see Grandpa's tiny world of watch parts I stand and look down over the edge of his high table. A ledge keeps the itty-bitty screwdrivers, wheels and gears from falling off. There are clock

parts in baby-food jars with the labels scrubbed
off and plain white ones glued on. He twirls
a steel tea bag full of clock parts in a jar of
foul-smelling liquid.

While waiting for Ernie Gene, I overhear
the strangest conversation. Aunt Holly walked
over to Dad behind the library wall and says,
"Louise is sure lucky to have you, Steve."

"I think I'm pretty lucky to have her,"
Dad said.

Aunt Holly gasps and looks stricken, like
she was just slapped.

****

Staying on the sidewalk, Ernie Gene and I
walk our bikes past the plastic Jesus, past the barber's pole. For a way down Main Street, we look
at Christmas in the store windows.

"So, what happened last night?" I ask. "You
were there, then you were gone."

He doesn't look at me. He backs away,
taking his bike with him. Stopping, with his back
against the wall, he shoves his hands into his
jacket pockets. "Coldest ride I've ever had! No
coat! No shoes!"

"But what happened?" I walk toward him with my bike, narrowing the space he had made between us. I touch his jacket.

He won't look me in the eye. "Coldest I've ever been! I rode all the way home freezing my buns off in the back of that pickup!" He turns away. "They just snatched me up and threw me in. Never said a word to me."

The Perm

chapter 15

Ernie Gene tries to save me. He says to his mother, "Let me show her my room."

"Ivy saw your room yesterday," Aunt Holly says. "Now shut up and get."

I climb into Aunt Holly's beauty shop chair. It might as well have been the electric chair. "Can you do a spiral perm?" I ask.

"Oh, no." She flings a plastic cape around my neck.

I clutch my hands together under it. I'm glad Aunt Holly can't see how nervous I am.

"I don't have the curlers for that."
She pulls over a basket on wheels full of colored curlers and talks.

I start out listening but loose track.

While she talks, Aunt Holly rolls wet paper-wrapped hunks of my hair around purple curlers. She snaps each one tight to my scalp. Then she dabs them all with a cotton ball oozing with a rotten smelling liquid. She tosses me a towel to deal with the acid juice threatening to drip onto my face. It slides toward my eyes. Maybe I cannot stop it. She is pulling my hair out, and she never stops talking.

After last night, I feel confused. How can she act so nice and be such a mess? I'm afraid to say anything for fear of setting her off. But I can tell she is going to talk all the way through the permanent. Finally, I get so frustrated I blurt out, "What happened last night?"

She mutters, "Oh, just a little Texas go-around," then goes on talking.

I try to listen, but I can't pay attention. At first, I think it's that I can't trust her. I go deaf when I can't trust who's talking to me. Whatever. Then I only want to know why. I keep asking my-self, why can she not answer me? Then I know. Fear. She's afraid of me. She's afraid to talk to me--a kid. Aunt Holly is afraid of other things, too. Lots of things. I don't know how I know this, but I do.

I can see her pain. She's hurt all over be-cause she hates so much. Against my will, I feel sorry for her. She reminds me of Boss Hogg, the sheriff of Hazard. He can't forgive the Duke boys. Then Bo says, "Keep that forgive and forget attitude!"

What? me forgive and forget? I don't think so. Even if I could forgive, I want to be sure and remember this,so I won't ever be like Aunt Holly.

Dear Lord, please don't let me grow up and accidentally be like Aunt Holly!

"Tilt you head back." Aunt Holly pours stuff over my curlers. The smell's awful. I hope it's not what Grandpa washes his clock parts in. It smells worse. Aunt Holly chats on and on, a disembodied voice behind me, around me, inside me, while the room fills with gas. Poisonous gas! Maybe the voice that drones on and on would get the stuff in my eyes. Blind me! On purpose! Or, even worse-

"Farrah?" Aunt Holly looms over me. "Farrah Fawcett?" You DO know who Farrah Fawcett is, don't you?"

"Oh, yes." I know who she is: one of Charlie's Angles. I'm not sure if I want to look like her, or Daisy Duke from my favorite TV show, **The Dukes of Hazard**. In fact, some things about being a girl is absolutely too silly. Like having your eyebrows tattooed on. Or your navel pierced. In school, even wearing pink is iffy. Or pretty shoes you can't run in. I know I have to draw the line somewhere; I just don't know exactly where, until Aunt Holly spins me around and

I behold in the mirror the Once and Future Me.
Forget Farrah! Forget Daisy! A pale face and eyes
wide with horror stare back at me. I look more
like the old-time kid film star—Shirley Temple.

"Oh, my goodness!"

That's just great! Life in sixth grade is
hard enough without looking like Shirley Temple. I'll be Little Miss Poufy Head to the kids at
school. Grandpa and Ernie Gene will never
take me seriously again!

The Last Christmas

chapter 16

After breakfast, a grim bunch waits for the festivities to begin. My family, Aunt Holly and Uncle Conner drop on the green couch. Ernie Jean and Skoshi make a solemn pair in the green chair. Dad is pouring coffee. Mom and Grandpa are having the most fun of all. They whisper and giggle like two kids. I snag a chair at the table next to Grandpa. He pokes me in the ribs with his elbow and says, "Hell's Bell!" as my grandmother glitters into the room.

Grandpa turns his back to them and hands me a silver dollar. "It's as old as you are, Ivy Calloway," he says, raising his voice to be heard over the radio music. He also gives me a turquoise ring he made in his shop. I put it on my finger at once.

Grandmother had piled her hair on top of her head and twisted little ringlets that hung down. Her eyes sparkle, her face is pink. She is pretty again. She smiles and chatters as she passes out presents. She hands Mom and Aunt Holly small boxes. They open to find crystal rings just like my grandmother wears.

Mom smiles and puts her ring on. So does Aunt Holly. Then they both hold their hands up to match my grandmother's crystal ring, and we all say hurray.

Teah would say it's some bonding ritual. I sure hope it's not. I don't like the idea of my mom connected to those two in any way. Mom winks at me.

Is this all pretend?

"To Ivy Calloway, from Santa." Grandmother hands me a stuffed doll wearing a fluffy pink dress.

I don't want to touch the thing, but I do. The doll has an evil face. She has tight stitches around her squinty eyes, a bunched-up nose, pooch cheeks, and a mouth that's a sucked-up scowl. The ears are little squashed knots. It looks like somebody pulled all the threads too tight. I tuck it behind the green chair.

I can see more unopened presents under the tree for me. If they're from my grandmother, I'm not so sure I want to open them. I settle back in my chair next to Grandpa and twirl my silver dollar. I watch how the light shines from Grandpa's ring. I watch everybody in the room tear open their presents. The lights twinkle. Skoshe is all over the place running with ribbons and bows.

Uncle Conner hands my grandmother a large box. "Open this first, Granny," he grins.

She rips off the paper and tears into the present like a kid. Then she shrieks, "You remembered! I can't believe you went back and bought it!"

It is a red, Indiana Jones hat, a hero's hat, and an adventurer's hat, with a crease and a wide brim. Grandmother cocks it this way and that, over one eye, then the other.

"A fedora," Dad says to me.

It's scary how easily I could be won over by my grandmother before she starts being weird again.

She struts around the room and checks herself in all twelve mirrors. The "Christmas Waltz" comes on the radio and she and Uncle Conner start dancing fancy ballroom stuff.

Only Aunt Holly watches grandmother and Uncle Conner as they whirl around.

Grandpa Boots gives Dad a gold chunk ring. And Mom's gift is a ruby necklace and stones to make rings. The precious stones folded in stiff paper don't look like much to me. But Mom acts sure proud of them.

The dance goes on. All this time Grandmother and Uncle Conner get louder and louder. They jump and rattle furniture. They twirl and stomp.

"When-e-e!" My grandmother makes little squeals and happy sounds. I think she turned weird awfully early in the day. I feel too embarrassed to watch them anymore. Grandpa ignores them completely and just talks to Mom. Aunt Holly wanders off. Dad is up for more ham. Ernie Gene still opens presents, and Skoshi has a ribbon.

Did someone turn up the music?

Grandpa and Mom lean closer so they can hear each other. They're almost yelling. Mom laughs into his ear. Grandpa cups his hands and shouts back into hers, "I wish you a Merry Christmas!"

"Dip!" Uncle Conner says at the same time. He and Grandmother pass by, traveling fast. He stops and leans her over backwards. She closes her eyes. Her little curls jiggle.

Skoshi barks.

Grandmother comes up giggling. Her face is red. Then away they go again.

"Hey, Old Man!" Aunt Holly appears in the kitchen doorway, both hands on her hips. "Old Man," she calls out. "It's Christmas, and you're not dead! The doctor was wrong. What do you think about that?"

Why does Aunt Holly sound so mean? Is she fixin' to yell some more? Would she yell at me? Throw furniture? Demand I commit suicide?

Grandpa doesn't seem to hear Aunt Holly. He doesn't look around at her. He keeps right on telling Mom probably the funniest story of her life, by the way she is laughing.

I catch Mom's eye, and she motions me over. "Go pack your suitcase," she whispers, "We're busting out of here. I can't believe we're not gone already!"

Of all the Christmas wishes, that one sounds the most beautiful.

I watch as Grandmother gathers my unopened presents into a Christmas bag.

The Road Home

chapter 17

Mom starts washing dishes and gives me the high sign. Ernie Gene and I dash out back. I hook Skoshi to her stakeout chain, and she takes a farewell pee. I scoop the last of her poop in a plastic bag and toss the whole thing in the garbage. Done with that.

"Here" My cousin hands me a joke book he bought at the museum. "I want you to remember. Remember me."

I hear Mom rattling dishes and running water in the kitchen with a fury. She wants out of here as much as I do.

A little after noon, Dad and I load up the van. Grandmother hands me a bag of all my unopened presents, along with some Christmas candy.

"I think we have everything, Mother," Mom stands on the porch almost smiling. She says to Grandmother, "If I've forgotten anything, just keep it. It's not important and don't worry about it."

Grandpa walks up beside Dad and says, "Steve, we'll meet y'all at Bubba's Texaco going west out of town. Filler up there and it'll take y'all half way home. Hey! Wait! I'll just show ya'. We'll meet ya'll there. Follow us!"

Grandmother nods and blots her faucet eyes. Then she stretches her fingers and squeezes them back again. Like she's saying that little kid's poem,

Open them! Shut them! Give a little clap!

Except, instead of a clap, my grandmother reaches for Mom, and they hug.

Open them! Shut them! Put them in your lap!

Some nerve! My grandmother wants a big hug. She and Mom are standing on the porch inside this huge holly wreath looking like a Christmas card. Grandmother finishes hugging quickly so she can wave at a car passing by.

I put the bike in the van first, then the pink doll and my bag of unopened presents. Stuff I'd just as soon leave there.

We go through the whole goodbye thing again at the gas station. As we head east, we wave good-bye to my grandmother, Grandpa and Ernie Gene. I watch as they become smaller and smaller. I watch until they are just dots. Then the grandpa dot starts jumping up and down. He flaps his arms. I see him shout, but it's too late. I cannot hear him. Grandmother gives him something and his fists pound the air. His arms and legs fly as he starts to run after us.

"Stop the van!" I shout. "It's Grandpa! He's running after us!"

Dad swerves the van to a stop. He drives backwards slowly. When a stumbling Grandpa catches up with us, I open the back door.

"Bell said that Lulu really needs these things bad!" He chokes for breath and grabs his pocket for a pill. He hands Mom a crumpled bag which she hands to me.

I take out Skoshi's stakeout chain and bowls. I forgot! Grandpa ran all this way because of me. Isn't Grandpa Boots sick? I try not to cry.

My grandmother drives up behind us. "Get in this car now! You ol' fool! Are you trying to kill yourself? I told you I could mail them to Lulu."

"No point if I can just give 'um to her right now."

Mom hugs Grandpa again. "I love you, Daddy."

"Love ya', too, cupcake."

Mom grins and shakes her head.

Was that whole deal just for Grandpa to get another hug from Mom?

Then she says to my grandmother, "No need to kill him right in front of me, Mother, I'm not coming back. Goodbye." Mom says with finality as she shuts the van door.

Grandpa gets in his car, we all wave goodbye again. I catch the expression on my grandmothers' face. Like a flash from a strobe light, it's a look I would see afterward when I closed my eyes. My grandmother is lost. Like a little girl lost, all her pain is just out there. I feel sorry for her. Yes, it's a pity. But could I forgive her? I don't know about that. I only know I can't hate her.

For the last time, we pass the school, Grandpa's shop, Ernie Gene's room. I would never again see the plastic baby Jesus wrapped in tinsel and laying in a matchstick manger.

The road out of town gives a peek at the little wooden houses around the cotton gin. Every roof is covered with snow. The trees are white with it. Snow sticks here and there to the bare ground. It piles up against fences. I feel hope and joy stir in my heart. I want to write a poem. "When did it snow?" I ask. I hear a whine in my voice. My feelings toss between happiness and sorrow. My white Christmas and I'd completely missed it.

"Cotton," Mom gulps in air like she'd been holding her breath. "Not snow. The farmers bring their cotton to the gin. It's the last of the cotton harvest. Cotton floats in the air and settles on houses, trees and fences. It only looks like snow."

"Things are not always as they seem, huh, Mom?"

Dad picks up speed. The earth unravels around us. Cotton Moon would soon be no more than a fleck in the rearview mirror. No regrets would ever come down that road for me. I'm already putting away my grandmother.

"She's a witch!" I blurt out. "A card-carry-ing, broom-toting witch!" I don't want to forget. "Sorry, Mom. I can't help it. I didn't want to be the one to tell you."

"I already know." Mom twists my grand-mother's ring. "She's always been. But this time she was the worst ever. I hopped she would be different for you, Ivy." Mom turns her face to the window. Her eyes focus on the horizon like some-thing there is of the keenest interest to her.

"She ruined Christmas!" I say. My stomach hurts. I feel bad all over.

Mom turns and smiles. She pulls Grand-mother's ring off and plops it into her purse. "But she doesn't have to ruin the rest of our lives."

"Do we ever have to go back there?"

"Never," she says. "Are you all right with that?"

"Sure. It's the Eighties, Mom. I'm a modern girl. But it's too bad this story doesn't have a happy ending. I might have to write it up for an English assignment...
What I Did for the Christmas Holidays"

She reaches over the front seat and hugs me. She kisses me on the top of my head. "Oh, those curls!" Her arms snuggle around them. "I have my happy ending. I carry it around with me. I wouldn't go anywhere without it."

"Silly Rabbit, you're the happy ending," Dad says. "And, oh, by the way. That phone call for you just before we left Fort Worth was from Jason. He wants to start running with you again right after Christmas.

There it is. My happy ending. It's been there all the time.

I spy a coffee can with a big red bow on it wedged in the back of the van.

"What's this?" A small branch pokes out of the can with one blooming yellow flower. "I don't remember packing this."

The card reads: "To Ivy Callaway, a rose for my little Rosebud. This is the Lady Banks rose, better known in these parts as The Yellow Rose of Texas. Plant it in the sun and remember that your old Paps loves ya'."

I hug the coffee can. This rose would be planted in the ground under my window. A rasping sound shakes from me, and I sob, "We never went fishing."

The blue van plunges down into the canyon. My ears pop. No mere ghost or spirit could ever scare me now. I had met my grandmother.

Then comes the long road with no radio, but we don't care. We sing what we know of M. C. Hammer's song, "You Can't Touch This!" *You can do this, and you can do that, but as for what I've got inside, you can't touch this!* We shout loud enough to rock the van.

We are planning to stop again at the Green Lizard Restaurant. This time, the sun sets behind us. I see the wooden bridge from a long way down the road.

I couldn't believe my eyes. That same boy I'd seen days before is fixin' to cross the bridge, too. His brown leather fringe from his jacket sways as he walks barefooted along the dusty road. He's carrying something, a little sister. Neither of them wears shoes.

That's it! I have an idea. If I don't want this grandmother, I shouldn't keep her presents. They make my stomach hurt, anyway. But not Grandpa's ring and the yellow rose. I'll keep them forever. I had wished for a grandmother with a pile of unopened presents. If I do my idea now, I'll be looking at a Christmas with no gifts from her. And that's great with me.

"Mom! Mom!" I shout. "Please, let me out right here. There are no cars. I can ride my bike over the bridge and meet y'all at the Green Lizard Restaurant."

Mom gives me a funny look, but Dad stops the van. I grab the doll and my Christmas bag, jump out of the van and hop on my bike. I catch up with the boy.

"Here," I say. "This is for you." I fling my Christmas bag full of Grandmother's unopened presents over his arm. He puts the little girl down. I hand the doll to her.

She gazes at the doll cuddled in her arms. "What a pretty face."

With one quick move, I turn. I mount my bike and pump. I feel a hundred pounds lighter, like I'm a feather. What did I need with a room full of unopened presents anyway? I toss away the dream of having another grandmother. Who needs that either?

I cross the bridge then head toward the Green Lizard Restaurant.

I do a little tap dance in the parking lot. Something good has happened to me. I'm not the same as I was.

At school I won't care if Michael and Jason sing "Come and Knock on My Door" for Amy all day long. I'm coming down out of that oak tree. Jason and I will be running together again. I have much. Skoshi. My Mom and Dad. And best of all, I have all the grandmothers I ever need or want. I feel good, and happy and wise as Teah.

THE BEGINNING